Birthday Surprise

For Tula Knowles,

a perfect angel

ALADDIN

An imprint of Simon & Schuster Children's Publishing Division
1230 Avenue of the Americas, New York, NY 10020
First Aladdin paperback edition June 2016
Originally published in Great Britain by Simon & Schuster UK, Ltd.
Text copyright © 2013 by Michelle Misra and Linda Chapman
Interior illustrations copyright © 2013 by Samantha Chaffey
Cover illustration copyright © 2016 by Christina Forshay
Also available in an Aladdin hardcover edition.
All rights reserved, including the right of reproduction in whole or in part in any form.
ALADDIN is a trademark of Simon & Schuster, Inc., and related logo is a registered trademark of Simon & Schuster, Inc.
For information about special discounts for bulk purchases, please contact
Simon & Schuster Special Sales at 1-866-506-1949 or business@simonandschuster.com.
The Simon & Schuster Speakers Bureau can bring authors to your live event.
For more information or to book an event contact the Simon & Schuster Speakers Bureau at 1-866-248-3049 or visit our website at www.simonspeakers.com.
Designed by Karina Granda
The text of this book was set in Bembo STD.
Manufactured in the United States of America 0516 OFF
2 4 6 8 10 9 7 5 3 1
Library of Congress Control Number 2016935277
ISBN 978-1-4814-5801-6 (hc)
ISBN 978-1-4814-5800-9 (pbk)
ISBN 978-1-4814-5802-3 (eBook)

ANGEL WINGS

Book #2: Birthday Surprise

by **MICHELLE MISRA**

illustrated by **SAMANTHA CHAFFEY**

ALADDIN

New York London Toronto Sydney New Delhi

Archangel
Grace

Jess

Primrose

CONTENTS

The
Guardian Angel
Academy
Third-Grade
Fireworks
Show

CHAPTER 1

An Important Announcement

WHAT'S GOING ON?" ELLA BROWN fluttered down the spiral staircase at the Guardian Angel Academy, coming to land at the bottom next to her friend, Tilly. The hallway was crammed full of angels gathered around a sign, and excited chatter filled the air. *Something* was definitely happening!

"Come and look at this!" Tilly pulled Ella through the crowd. "Excuse me! Excuse me, please," she said to the other angels until they reached the front.

The sign was glittery and sparkly and kept changing color. "*The Guardian Angel Academy Third-Grade Fireworks Show*," Ella read aloud. "*Friday the twenty-fifth of October.* Oh, angel-tastic!" she exclaimed, pushing her dark brown hair behind her ears. "We're having a fireworks show in three days."

"I know!" said Tilly, her eyes shining. "It's the day our parents come to take us home for the midterm break."

Ella clutched her arm. "Look—the paper's changing again!" They watched excitedly as the paper turned purple.

Tilly read the words. "*All third-grade angels will be expected to take part in the show.*"

Ella caught her breath. "So we're all going to actually *perform* in the fireworks show?"

"Yes, indeed," came a voice from behind them. Everyone swung around. Angel Seraphina, Ella and Tilly's class tutor, was standing there. "Every third-grade angel will get a turn at carrying the different lights through the sky, and the very best angel will get a starring role in the finale."

"Oh, halos and wings!" breathed Ella.

"That would be really scary," said Tilly, her eyes wide.

"It would be amazing!" said Ella, imagining everyone watching her as she swooped and dived, setting off fireworks in the sky.

"One thing's for sure, you're all going to have fun whether you have a starring role or not." Angel Seraphina smiled. "And I'm sure your parents will enjoy watching the show, before taking you home for the midterm break. However, if you want that starring role you'd better practice your flying." Angel Seraphina flew away.

Ella turned to Tilly. "I've seen a fireworks show before, but to actually take part in one—maybe have the main part—wouldn't that be *totally glittery*!"

"I wouldn't get too excited, Ella Brown," came a haughty voice from behind them.

"It's not likely *you'll* get the starring role, is it?"

Ella turned and saw Primrose standing there. She was the most annoying angel in the whole school. With her sparkling blue eyes, and pretty blonde hair curled into ringlets, she looked perfectly angelic—but she so wasn't.

Ella felt Tilly shrink back—Tilly hated arguments—but *she* wasn't scared of Primrose. "And why shouldn't I get the starring role?" she demanded.

"Didn't you hear what Angel Seraphina said?" Primrose nudged the angel standing beside her, who had red hair and giggled when prompted. "Only the *best* angel will get the starring role. And one thing's for certain—you *definitely* don't fall into that category." Her eyes swept snootily over Ella. "All you're best at is getting into trouble!"

Ella put her hands on her hips. "You've been sent to the Sad Cloud as often as me, Primrose."

"Ella, don't get into an argument now," Tilly pleaded, tugging her arm. "You heard what Angel Seraphina said—everyone will get to take part in the show. It doesn't really matter who has the starring role."

"Come on, Veronica." Primrose turned to her friend. "We've got better things to do with our time than stand around talking to troublemakers like Ella." And with that she flounced off.

"Right! That's it!" Ella sprang after her.

Tilly grabbed her. "No, Ella! Ignore her.

She's just trying to make you mad so you get into trouble."

Ella stopped herself. Tilly was right. Primrose loved to make her lose her temper—usually when there was a teacher around. Angels were *never* supposed to lose their temper. It said so in the handbook that all the third-grade angels had been given a copy of. "All right, I won't go after her," said Ella, "but she is just so annoying! I hope she doesn't get the starring role in this show." *And I hope I do,* she added to herself.

"Forget Primrose," said Tilly. "Let's find the others and tell them all about the fireworks show."

Ella and Tilly hurried outside into the court-yard, where they found Poppy and Jess, their other two best friends, sitting underneath the marble statue of their founder, Archangel Emmanuel. Jess was bouncing a ball back and forth against a wall and they were sharing cloudberry cookies, their white halos gleaming in the sun. Archangel Emmanuel had been sculpted in full song, mouth open, eyes wide. It was one of Ella's favorite statues in the school grounds.

"Where have you two been?" Poppy asked. As usual, her curly blonde hair looked like a bird had been nesting in it and the rest of her looked just as messy—her white dress even had a splotch of sauce from breakfast! Jess was much neater—her dark hair was tied back in a ponytail, and her uniform was clean.

"We've been finding out something very exciting," said Ella. "Now," she pretended to tease, "shall we tell them, Tilly? Or shall we not?"

"Tell us!" said Poppy eagerly.

"Well . . . guess what *we'll* be doing in three days," said Ella.

"What?" Poppy said.

"Only performing in a fireworks show!" Ella exclaimed. She quickly explained about the sign.

"Oh, glittersome!" exclaimed Poppy.

"Just think how totally sparkly it will be to take part in a fireworks show," enthused Tilly.

Ella looked at Jess. The dark-haired angel was sitting quietly. "It's really exciting, isn't it, Jess?" Ella said, surprised her friend hadn't said anything.

"Yeah . . . yeah, sure it is," muttered Jess. Ella frowned. Jess didn't sound that excited. But then Jess was kind of shy—maybe she didn't like the idea of performing in front of everyone.

Before Ella could ask her if that was what it was, the school bell rang. "Time to go," said Tilly, pulling Poppy up. "We don't want to be late for class."

A bluebird who had been circling around the head of the statue swooped down and pecked up the crumbs from their cloudberry cookies. His coat shone in different shades of indigo and turquoise and his dark eyes sparkled like jewels.

"Look at him. Isn't he beautiful!" said Tilly.

"Bluebirds are supposed to be lucky," commented Ella.

"He'll be very *unlucky* for us if looking at him makes us late for Angel Gabriella's class!" said Tilly, setting off. "Come on, all of you! I don't want to lose any halo stamps today."

Halo stamps were what you earned for good behavior and all of the angels at the Academy had halo cards for them. This being their first year, the third graders had been told that when they filled up their card, the color of their halo and uniform would change, and their wings would grow a bit bigger. All the third graders still had the white halos and white dresses they had started with at the beginning of term a few weeks ago, but the next level up was a sparkling sapphire-blue, and they all wanted to change to that. But they had to be careful—halo stamps could also be taken away for lateness, untidiness, and generally behaving in ways that angels shouldn't.

"How many halo stamps have you all got now?" Poppy asked.

"Four," said Tilly.

"Four! That's fabulous," said Poppy. "I've got three."

"Well, I've only got two," sighed Ella.

"You would have had three if you hadn't had one taken away for that flying tangle with Primrose last month," Tilly pointed out.

"True," Ella said. "What about you, Jess? Jess . . . ?" Ella looked around. Jess was still standing at the foot of the statue, lost in thought. "Jess, come on!" Ella went back for her. "What are you doing? You should be coming to class with us."

"Oh, sorry," Jess said distractedly. "I was just thinking about something."

"Is it the fireworks show?" Ella asked. "Are you worried about performing?"

Jess looked suprised. "Oh no, I'm not worried about that. I wouldn't want a main part anyway. It'll be nice just being in the background."

"Oh. So what's the matter?" Ella said.

"I'm fine. Nothing's the matter. Nothing at all." Jess quickly flew after the others.

Ella frowned as she watched her go. Jess could say what she liked, but she was beginning to feel sure something was up with her friend. What could it possibly be?

CHAPTER 2

Heavenly Animals

THE FOUR ANGELS FLUTTERED ACROSS the courtyard and flew into the hallway on the opposite side. It was a tall room, covered from wall to ceiling with iridescent moons and stars. Two chandeliers dangled from the ceiling, sparkling like diamonds, and making it look like the most magical starry night ever.

"Come on," said Tilly, speeding up. All of the third-grade angels' flying had improved loads since they had started at the school a few

weeks ago. "You all go on ahead," called Jess. "I want to check the mail room first."

"Why?" said Ella, stopping, her wings fluttering.

The mail pigeons only delivered once a day and the four of them had already checked the pigeonholes that morning.

Jess shrugged. "I just do."

"I'll come with you then," Ella offered. Leaving Tilly and Poppy to fly on, she followed Jess into the mail room. There was a row of pigeonholes made out of shining gold. Each student had their own pigeonhole with their name written underneath it in sparkling sapphires. By the window, the mail pigeons perched on jeweled stands. The pigeons had their heads tucked under their golden wings, resting before they set off to get more mail that evening. There were a few older angels also checking their pigeonholes. Jess checked hers. As Ella had suspected, it was still empty.

"Are you expecting something, Jess?" one of the older angels asked.

"Yes," sighed Jess.

"Me too." The angel shrugged. "I've been waiting for days. There are quite a few of us who seem to be missing packages. Isn't it strange?"

Jess nodded. "I was sure there would be something here. . . ."

"What are you expecting?" Ella asked her curiously.

"It's not important," said Jess, swallowing hard and flying out of the room.

Ella flew after her. "But—"

"I don't want to talk about it, Ella!" Jess said sharply.

Ella blinked. Jess never snapped. What was the matter with her? She wanted to ask more but she didn't want to upset Jess, so she decided to keep quiet. They flew to the second floor where the maze of hallways divided off, leading to different classrooms. As they neared the room where their heavenly animals class was taking place, a loud, unmistakable voice floated out. Primrose!

"Another halo stamp for neatness," she was saying smugly. "I've got seven now. It's only to be expected, of course! I am always so neat and tidy."

"Not always very modest though," Ella muttered under her breath. They flew in to find Primrose showing everyone the holographic stamp that Angel Gabriella had just awarded her.

"All right, angels, settle down," said Angel Gabriella. "Ella . . . Jess . . . you got here just in time. Take your places quickly please and let's get started." Angel Gabriella always reminded Ella of a bun—she was very round and had black eyes just like little currants. They were usually kind and twinkly, but she didn't tolerate any nonsense.

"Over here, Ella," called Tilly, indicating the spaces that

she and Poppy had saved for them at a table. There were pads of paper and paint out for all the angels. Ella felt excited. They didn't usually do art in their heavenly animals class, but she loved drawing and painting.

"This looks fun! What does Angel Gabriella want us to do today?" whispered Ella, grabbing a jar of glittery paint, a brush, and some water before sitting herself down in the chair beside Tilly and leaning over her paper.

"We've each got to choose a different heavenly animal to paint," Tilly whispered back. "I'm painting a phoenix. What will you do?"

"I'll try a winged horse," said Ella. Happiness sparkled through her. Lost in her painting, her hands flew over the page, flicking this way and that as she dipped her brush in and out of the dish of water. Finally, she stopped and looked up.

"Let's see," said Tilly.

Ella turned the pad around.

"Oh Ella, it's amazing!" said Tilly.

"What's amazing?" Primrose came over.

"Look!" Tilly said, placing the pad back down on the table.

Primrose moved dangerously close to the dish of water. "Hmm, let me see."

Tilly grabbed the dish of water just before Primrose spilled it.

"Whoops, silly me," said Primrose, arching her eyebrows. "I wouldn't want to ruin your lovely painting, Ella." She reached out for the picture again, this time her elbow catching intentionally against a jar of blue paint.

"Careful!" Jess gasped, grabbing the jar before it could spill all over Ella's picture.

"Thanks, Jess," said Ella quickly.

"Oh, dearie me, I am being clumsy today," said Primrose.

"Look, Primrose, can you just go away?" Ella said through gritted teeth. She glanced over and saw Angel Gabriella look in their direction.

"But I'm only trying to look at your picture," said Primrose innocently.

"You're not," hissed Ella. "You're trying to ruin it!"

Primrose pretended to look shocked. "Me? I wouldn't do a thing like that!"

"What's going on here?" Angel Gabriella came over. "Is there a problem, angels?"

"No, no problem, Angel Gabriella." Primrose smiled sweetly. "Ella just seems to think I want to ruin her painting, but of course I'd never do anything like that. Angels must never be mean," she quoted from the school handbook. "I just wanted to admire Ella's beautiful painting."

"That's lovely of you, dear. Now, let me see, Ella," said Angel Gabriella. "Oh, it is rather good, isn't it?" Her face broke into a big, beaming smile. "I think a picture like that definitely deserves a halo stamp." With a tap from her wand, a glitter of sparkles spun out over Ella's card and the most beautiful holographic stamp appeared on it.

Ella beamed.

"Thank you for pointing Ella's picture out

to me, Primrose," said Angel Gabriella. "That was very kind of you. Now Ella, if only you could apply yourself as well to your punctuality as you do to your drawing, you'd be the perfect angel!" She swept on to see what the rest of the class were doing. To Ella's relief, Primrose moved away, looking annoyed. She put her picture down. Then she noticed that Jess was staring glumly at her own picture.

"So how are you doing, Jess?" said Ella, going over to her. "What have you drawn?"

Jess sighed. "It's not very good."

"Let me see."

It was a bluebird like the one outside, only its legs were a little long, the beak was a little wonky, and the wings were more like the size of an eagle's.

"It's beautiful, Jess," said Ella kindly.

"You know it's not," Jess sighed. "Can you help me?"

"Well, if you change the legs a little like this"—Ella picked up her brush—"and add a little more here." She rubbed out a little on the right. . . . Finally she had finished.

"It's perfect now, Ella." Jess grinned.

"It really is. It's just like the sweet bluebird by the statue," Poppy agreed, coming around and looking at it too.

"Not all bluebirds are sweet, you know." Archangel Gabriella joined in, overhearing the conversation in passing. "They can be mischievous birds as well. Haven't you heard about the time a bluebird took Archangel Grace's brooch? They love all sorts of glittery things, and nest in the strangest places." The teacher smiled and headed off to join another group of angels.

"So what's going on here?" It was Primrose again.

"Oh, not you again, Primrose," sighed Ella.

"Well that's not very friendly, is it?" Primrose said, looking hurt. "And there I was, coming over to see how Jess was doing as well. So what have you drawn, Jess? Oh!" Her eyes widened. "It's a blue pelican!"

Jess's face crumpled.

It was the final straw for Ella. Annoying her was one thing, but teasing one of her friends was quite another. Her temper snapped and, before she could stop herself, she had picked up the blue jar of paint and spilled it all over Primrose!

Primrose shrieked.

"Ella! What have you done?" cried Jess, covering her mouth as Poppy and Tilly both gasped in horror.

Hearing all the commotion, Angel Gabriella turned. "Angels! What *is* happening?" she cried, as Primrose stood there, blue paint dripping down her face and onto the floor.

CHAPTER 3

Missing Mail

OH NO! ELLA CRINGED AS SHE LOOKED at her furious teacher. What had she done?

"Oh, Angel Gabriella!" wailed Primrose. "Ella spilled the jar of paint on me—and look at the mess on the floor as well." She sobbed loudly and dramatically.

"Did you? Did you, Ella? Did you really do this?" demanded Angel Gabriella.

"I ... um ... I did," admitted Ella, her mouth feeling dry. "I'm sorry. I shouldn't have done

it, I know," she rushed on. "But Primrose was being rude about Jess's picture and—"

"That is enough!" snapped Angel Gabriella. "There can be no excuse for spilling paint on people. It is abominable behavior! That halo stamp I gave you will have to be taken back!"

"I'm very sorry, Angel Gabriella," said Ella, hanging her head. "I'll clean up the mess."

"You most certainly will," said Angel

Gabriella. "And after that you can take yourself off to the Sad Cloud, where you can stay until you've had time to think about what you've done. I'm very disappointed in you."

Ella groaned inwardly. She hated the fact that Angel Gabriella was disappointed and, although she knew that she deserved it, she hated her punishment. The Sad Cloud was the most boring place ever—there was nothing to do there but read old books on angel history and angel rules. Still, there wasn't a thing she could do about it now. No matter how annoying Primrose had been, she shouldn't have spilled paint on her.

Angel Gabriella turned to Primrose. "Take yourself outside, Primrose, and get cleaned up. Veronica can go with you."

Sobbing as loudly as she could and glaring at

Ella, Primrose left the classroom with Veronica. Ella didn't dare to look at her friends. She got a mop and some water. Poppy, Jess, and Tilly all rushed to help her.

"No!" Angel Gabriella told them sharply. "Please leave Ella to clean up on her own. Bring your work over to this table."

Shooting Ella sympathetic looks, the other three had to do as they were told.

As she cleaned away the paint, Ella ranted at herself. How could she have done something so stupid? It was her awful temper. She was never going to be a good enough angel to be a Guardian Angel and, if she wasn't careful, all the other third-grade angels would fill their halo cards and get sapphire halos before her. She'd be the only one left with a white halo! Tears prickled in her eyes. What if Angel Gabriella decided she should be banned from the fireworks show as well? As soon as Ella had finished cleaning, she began to leave for the Sad Cloud. In the doorway she passed Primrose, coming back with Veronica.

"I'll get you back for that, Ella Brown!" hissed Primrose as she pushed past Ella, her elbows bumping Ella sharply in the ribs. "Just see if I don't."

Ella spent a very dull hour in the Sad Cloud on her own. The walls and floor were all painted gray and the seats were hard. She leafed through the books on the history of the school, but they weren't very exciting. In the end she sat down with a book and thought about her friends. She remembered how strange Jess had acted by the pigeonholes earlier. What was making her so unhappy? Ella thought about what Jess had said. She was obviously waiting for something to arrive, but what?

Ella started turning the pages of the book. The first chapter was about how the school was built. Her eyes read the words. *The school's official birthday is the first of January. . . .*

Birthday!

Of course! Ella realized something. It was Jess's birthday in two days—just before the end of term. She must have been checking the mail room to see if her parents had sent her anything yet!

Ella remembered what the older angels had

said about mail going missing. Maybe Jess's parents had sent her something and *that*, too, had gone missing.

Ella drew her knees up to her chest thoughtfully. Jess's birthday would be the first of her friends' birthdays at angel school. *We'll have to do something to celebrate,* she mused. *Especially if something is wrong with the mail and nothing arrives for Jess. We'll have to make it feel like a very special day. Tilly and Poppy and I can plan something!* Her eyes started to sparkle. *Oh yes, this is going to be fun!*

As soon as Angel Gabriella came and said Ella could leave the Sad Cloud, she set off to find her friends. It was lunchtime. As she hurried down the stairs and into the maze of hallways, she looked through each of the classroom windows—but they weren't there. They must have gone back to the dorm.

She flew up to the next floor and hurried off down the hallway that led to the turrets. As she flew, she whizzed past planets and stars covering the floors and ceilings, before coming to a halt just beside the mail room. She'd check one more time, just in case something had arrived for Jess after all.

As she started to peer around the door, something stopped her in her tracks—the sight of two people talking. It was Archangel Grace and the gardening teacher, Angel Celestine, and they were talking quite intently. The half-moon glasses on the end of Archangel Grace's nose were waggling as she spoke and her enormous gossamer wings were trembling in agitation.

"Whatever is going on, Celestine?" she was saying. "I don't understand it. Packages and letters keep disappearing. It's most puzzling."

"I know. . . ." Angel Celestine answered. "As far as I can tell, the pigeons are arriving with

☆ ☆ *37* ☆ ☆

the mail as usual, but then before anyone gets to their pigeonholes in the morning, things disappear, and often people who have been expecting packages and letters aren't getting them. I don't understand what's happening."

Archangel Grace looked grave. "It's clear that someone must be taking them."

Angel Celestine gasped. "But who would do such a thing?"

Ella sucked in her breath. Surely no angel would steal mail? She was horrified at the thought. But Archangel Grace was right—if packages were arriving and then disappearing someone had to be taking them.

"It simply must be one of the angels," Archangel Grace said, shaking her head. "I know it's hard to believe, but we must find the culprit."

"There you are!" A hand touched Ella's shoulder, making her nearly jump out of her skin.

"Tilly . . . Poppy . . ." Ella breathed, relieved that it was only her friends who had discovered her eavesdropping. "What are you doing here?"

"Looking for you, silly," said Tilly.

"Where's Jess?" Ella asked.

"She offered to help Angel Seraphina clean up our classroom," said Poppy.

"Fabulous!" said Ella, suddenly remembering what she had been thinking about in the Sad Cloud. "Then let's get to our dorm. I've got something I need to talk to you about and I don't want Jess to hear...."

CHAPTER 4

Flying Frenzy

JESS'S BIRTHDAY! HOW COULD WE ALL have forgotten?" Tilly and Poppy each sat on one of the little floating clouds that doubled as beds in their dorm.

"If there's a chance that Jess's mail *has* gone missing—that she's not going to get any birthday presents from her parents—then that's all the more reason to do something extra-special for her," said Poppy.

"But what?" wondered Tilly.

"Hmm." Ella frowned and looked around their dorm. It was a cozy room with a large oval window looking out over the grounds, and it had four white closets and four dressing tables, each with one of their names in large golden letters. "A party would be the obvious choice, but her birthday's Thursday and we've got fireworks show practice all day and then we're going home on Friday, so we won't have time for one."

"That's true," said Tilly.

"We need to think of something else," said Poppy.

They all racked their brains. But it wasn't so easy to think of something. What could they possibly do?

Soon, Jess joined them and the three friends had to stop talking about it. After lunch they had flying class. Now each and every one of them were able to raise themselves off the ground and fly around, but carrying lights for the fireworks show in their arms was a different matter. The third-grade angels soon found that it could really throw you off balance.

"That's it, Poppy," called out the flying teacher, Angel Raffaella. "Try to imagine your wings are like a butterfly's. Keep your arms still. Gently, easy does it."

"I'm trying," Poppy called through gritted teeth, as she managed to raise herself off the ground with a light in her hand and flutter into the sky, only to lose her balance and come crashing down again.

Ella concentrated on flying up high and, before she knew it, she was up, up, and away.

"Whoa!" she called, wobbling a bit as she clutched the light in one hand and tried to steer with the other arm.

"That's it, Ella, you're doing really well," encouraged Angel Raffaella.

☆ ☆ 45 ☆ ☆

Ella began to get the hang of it. She looked across the sky to see how everyone else was doing. Some of the angels were still stuck on the ground, while others were managing to raise themselves up, only to fall down again. Ella looked across and saw Primrose gliding smoothly across the sky, her ringlets flying out behind her, her light held securely in her hands. Angels and wings! Annoyingly, it looked like Primrose was rather good at flying carrying a light. Ella bit down on her tongue as she watched Primrose pirouetting around.

"Very good, Primrose," Angel Raffaella called after a while. "You're a natural. Now, I've had a chance to watch you all, so if you could gather around, I've got an announcement to make about the show."

One by one, the angels came back down before gathering in a group in front of Angel Raffaella. The flying teacher started.

"Well," she said, "as you know, I have been asked to make a choice on who should have the starring role at the fireworks show and, on the basis of today's class, I'd like to say that I've chosen"—she paused and smiled—"Primrose de-broe Ferguson."

"That's me! It's me!" Primrose could hardly contain herself. She jumped up and down—and then she seemed to remember herself. "Thank you, Angel Raffaella," she said meekly, clasping her hands together. "It is a complete honor to be chosen. I hope I will make you proud."

Angel Raffaella smiled warmly. "Very humbly spoken. What a good angel. I am sure you *will* make me proud, my dear."

Ella raised her eyebrows at her friends. Of all the angels, it just had to be Primrose who'd been chosen! But even she had to admit that the decision had been a fair one—Primrose had been the best in the class. As Angel Raffaella turned away, Ella forced herself to do the right thing and went over to congratulate Primrose. "Well done," she said.

"Told you I'd be the star!" Primrose crowed triumphantly. "And I hope you enjoy watching me, Ella Brown—from the back row!" She swept off, smirking in delight.

CHAPTER 5

Glitter Bomb!

O N THE WAY TO GLITTER CLASS LATER
that day, all Primrose could talk about
was having the starring role in the show. Ella
tried very hard to ignore her. There was no
way she wanted to get into trouble again.

Glitter class was great fun. They all had to
learn to make the glitter bombs that they were
going to set off as part of the fireworks show.

"I like your bomb, Ella," said Tilly, coming
over to inspect the big, colorful glitter bomb

Ella was making. Ella had sculpted the outside from papier-mâché, and was now filling it
with sparkles and streamers—all the things she
wanted to explode out of it into the sky.

"Are you ready for the special ingredient,
Ella?" Angel Gabriella came over and pulled
out a little bottle from her pocket, before sprin-
kling a little dust inside the glitter bomb. "Not

too much," she said, a twinkle in her eye. "We don't want too much of an explosion."

"So what's in it, Angel Gabriella?" asked Tilly curiously.

Angel Gabriella tapped the side of her nose. "Now that's a magic secret," she smiled. "Suffice to say, there's a whole lot of angel dust as part of the mix. Third graders just need to be able to make glitter bombs and not learn how to make them explode. Now, come on everyone, show me your bombs so I can add the magic to them too."

Angel Gabriella went around the rest of the class, tapping her little bottle into each of the glitter bombs before she finally placed the bottle back in a glass cabinet. Ella watched her closely before putting the lid on her glitter bomb, sealing it, and then covering it all over in red glitter and red hearts.

"That looks lovely, Ella," said Angel Gabriella, coming over.

"How do we make the glitter bombs go off?" Ella asked.

"Ah, more magic!" said Angel Gabriella. "Now, all of you put the lids on your glitter bombs and make a circle three times on the lids with your wands, saying:

Glitter bomb, listen to me
You will explode, on the count of three.

The angels all did as she said.

"Now, when it's time for the fireworks show and we want the glitter bombs to go off," Angel

Gabriella went on, "all you need to do is circle your wand three times in the air and count out loud to three. Each of you will make your own glitter bomb explode. We will practice it so you are all safely out of the way when the glitter bombs explode. The magic in them is powerful and you could get hurt if you were too close. Now, put your glitter bombs over there in the pile with the others, ready for Friday."

As Ella placed her bomb into the pile, a little idea started to grow in her mind. What if . . . ? What if she made a glitter bomb for Jess's birthday on Thursday? A really big one! That would be a cherub-tastic birthday surprise! She'd need to get some of Angel Gabriella's special powder. But it would only need a pinch—and it was for a good cause. It would make Jess's birthday really special.

She thought about the school handbook and recited one of the rules in her head: *Angels should always strive to make others happy.* That was what she would be doing. She grinned to herself. She couldn't wait to tell Poppy and Tilly!

As soon as class was over, Jess went to check the pigeonholes one more time. Ella was quick to grab Poppy and Tilly and pull them to one side.

"Quick—while Jess isn't here. I've got it," she said triumphantly. "I know exactly what we can do for Jess's birthday. Why don't we make a glitter bomb? The biggest and best glitter bomb ever!"

She looked eagerly at them. They both looked uncertain. "I don't know, Ella …" Poppy said, looking across at Tilly.

"I'm not sure about it either," said Tilly. "I mean, we're really only just beginners. What if it goes wrong?"

"It won't go wrong!" said Ella airily. "We just make a bomb, like we have just now but bigger, and sneak a tiny pinch of Angel Gabriella's magic dust, and that's it!"

"Well, you were pretty good at making your glitter bomb," Poppy said cautiously. "Especially considering it was only our first lesson. What do you think, Tilly?"

"Maybe it'll be okay," said Tilly. "Yes, all right, I'm sure it'll be fine. I mean, it should be pretty straightforward. But not a big bomb, just a little one."

Poppy nodded. "Tilly's right. It should just be a small glitter bomb that can be contained in our dorm, so if there's any mess or anything goes wrong we can clean it up."

"But a small glitter bomb's so boring," protested Ella.

"Ella . . ." her two friends said warningly.

"All right, all right," Ella sighed. "A small glitter bomb it is. This is going to be so much fun. I'll start designing and making it. Then all we have to do is get our hands on Angel Gabriella's special ingredient!"

The next day, they were so busy practicing for the fireworks show that Ella barely had enough time to even *think* about the glitter bomb, let alone make it! She enjoyed the practicing though. She was almost as good as Primrose at carrying things now. As soon as Jess went off to the school Music Club after dinner, Ella, Tilly, and Poppy hurried to their dorm and started to put the birthday glitter bomb together.

"What should we put in it?" asked Tilly.

"Definitely loads of glitter," said Ella. "And some magic sparkles too. Here, let me use my wand."

"Are you sure you should?" Tilly said, anxiously.

"It'll be fine," said Ella. "I know—what about glittery letters that spell out words?" She picked up her wand and thought for a moment before waving it in the air.

Conjure sparkly letters, a message to say:
Happy Birthday, Jess, on your special day.

"Oh, Ella, it's fabulous," cried Tilly as the letters *Happy Birthday, Jess!* appeared in large sparkly letters in the air.

"That's really clever," said Poppy, impressed. "You're so good at glitter magic, Ella!"

Feeling pleased with herself, Ella circled the letters with her wand and then tapped the glitter bomb and the letters. They popped inside the bomb, along with the other decorations, and Ella put the lid on.

"Now all we need is Angel Gabriella's special ingredient," said Poppy. "Who's going to get that?"

"I guess that should probably be me," said Ella, "seeing as it was my idea in the first place."

"Are you sure?" said Tilly, looking relieved.

"Yes, sure," said Ella. She picked up the bomb and covered it up with one of the dresses from her closet. Then, taking a look one way and then the other, Ella sneaked off down the hall with it in her arms. She was quiet as she flew, checking each of the classrooms. Most of the angels were in their dorms doing homework or at their after-school clubs.

Quickly, Ella raced down the hall, turning the corner before arriving at Angel Gabriella's room. Thankfully, the room was unlocked and she crept inside.

Tiptoeing over to the glass cabinet where she had seen Angel Gabriella put the special ingredient, she hesitated for a moment. What if it was locked? But to her relief she saw that

Angel Gabriella had left the little golden key in the lock. Gently Ella reached out and turned it. Phew! She was just about to take the bottle when she heard voices outside.

Quick as a flash, she jumped back behind the door, hugging the glitter bomb, her heart pounding. Thankfully, the footsteps passed on by. Ella waited until all was quiet and then she crept out again to the cabinet.

The red dust in the little bottle sparkled.

Ella took the bottle and pulled out the silver cork. She opened the bomb's lid and scattered a little inside—and then she stopped. How much did she need? It would be awful if it didn't go off! She put another big sprinkle into the bomb and was about to put the cork back in when she couldn't resist the temptation. She added another big sprinkle, just for luck. She knew Tilly and Poppy wanted a small glitter bomb, but where was the fun in that? She smiled to herself as she imagined Jess's stunned face as the bomb exploded. She was going to be so happy. Ella felt excitement bubble up through her. She simply couldn't wait for the next day! She loved making her friends happy.

Putting in the cork, she put the bottle back and locked the cabinet up. Then she cast the spell on the glitter bomb as Angel Gabriella had taught her and set off back to the dorm as fast as she could.

"Done it!" she cried cheerily, pushing back the door.

"That's fabulous, Ella," cried Poppy and Tilly.

"You did put only a little bit of the angel dust in though, didn't you?" Tilly asked anxiously.

"Yes, yes, just a little bit," lied Ella.

"So where shall we put it?" said Poppy, looking around the dorm.

"How about over the door," said Tilly.

"Great idea!" said Poppy. "Let's put it there now, then it will be ready for Jess tomorrow. We can set it off when we get back from assembly, before classes start. Ella, you can put a disguising spell on it so Jess won't notice."

"This is going to be just perfect!" Ella said happily, as she thought about all the angel dust inside the glitter bomb. "The best birthday surprise ever!"

CHAPTER 6

A Change of Plan

AS THE ANGELS SLEPT THAT EVENING, all was quiet, the sound of gentle breathing filling the dorm. But Ella couldn't sleep. She tossed and turned, her thoughts firmly on the glitter bomb. Surely they could do better than the door of their dorm, couldn't they? It seemed such a waste. There had to be another place for it to go off where *everyone* would see it. Then all the angels in the school would know it was Jess's birthday!

Ella's thoughts raced. Where else could she put it? Somewhere everyone would be when it went off. Suddenly an idea popped into her head. The statue of Angel Emmanuel! Everyone passed it on the way out of assembly in the morning. It was the perfect position. If she could make it explode from behind as everyone filed into the courtyard, then it would be amazing. . . .

She stopped herself. Tilly and Poppy would never agree to it. She bit her lip. Maybe . . . maybe she could put it by the statue without telling them. Okay, so they would be surprised, but they'd soon forgive her when they saw how perfect it was, wouldn't they? And when they saw Jess's face!

Yes, she'd do it. . . . Ella's mind was made up. First thing in the morning. She'd get up early, but for now it was time to get some rest. . . . And now that a plan was in place, Ella fell into a deep sleep.

When Ella woke a few hours later, the sun was just rising in the sky. The first thing she did was roll over and check the other cloud beds. They were moving gently around the room, but her friends were still quietly sleeping.

Quickly, Ella got out of bed and pulled on her clothes. Then she flew up and pulled the glitter bomb down.

All was quiet as she pushed open the door and flew along the hall, down the spiral staircase, and into the giant hallway.

She went out into the courtyard, the heavy door creaking slightly as she turned the big gold handle. The morning dew was fresh on

the ground and the rays of the early-morning
sun shone down. The bluebird was circling
around the statue's head again. Ella wondered
where his nest was—it must be nearby.

Putting her foot onto the angel statue, she
pushed herself up from the ground.

"Sorry about this, Archangel Emmanuel,"
she apologized to the statue as she climbed.

"I hope you don't mind me standing on you." Reaching up, she grabbed the angel's halo and used it to steady herself. Then she reached up and, carefully, very carefully, she placed the glitter bomb on the angel's shoulders before jumping back down to the ground to admire her handiwork. Last thing to do was cast a disguising spell so no one else would know it was there. She waved her wand:

Disguise and hide, true shape concealed,
Until it's time to be revealed.

She smiled as the bomb faded from sight. All was ready. *If this doesn't cheer Jess up,* she thought happily, *nothing will.*

☆ ☆ ☆

It was quiet and still as Ella let herself back into the school. A troubling thought crossed her mind. What if the others had woken up and found her gone? "I know, I'll check the mail room," she said to herself. "See if there's anything there for Jess yet. I can say that's where I've been."

She ran to the pigeonholes, quickly making her way over to Jess's, and peeped inside. She let out a heavy sigh. It was still empty. It made her surer than ever that her plan was the right one. Jess had no packages to open that morning, but at least she was going to get a great, big, angel surprise!

Ella was so impatient she could hardly eat any breakfast that morning and she fidgeted as they went in for assembly. Jess had run down to her pigeonhole first thing but found nothing there and was looking very sad. Ella, Poppy, and Tilly had sung "Happy Birthday" to her and given her cards they had made but, although Jess had smiled, she wasn't any happier by the time they went to assembly.

Ella couldn't wait for the glitter bomb to go off. As they waited for Archangel Grace to come onto the stage and talk to them all, she nudged Jess. "Cheer up!"

Jess forced a smile. "Sorry!"

"Shhh," came a pious voice from behind them.

"Oh, do be quiet, Primrose," Ella said impatiently. "It's Jess's birthday."

But there wasn't time to get into a fight now. Archangel Grace had come onstage and begun to speak.

"Good morning, angels," she said. "This morning we will be hearing from Polly and Chloe, who will be performing the Angelic Concerto Major in E flat." She nodded across at two angels who sat with their harps at the ready, looking nervous. "But before we do, I have a serious announcement to make. Some of you may already be aware, but it has come to my attention that over the last few days, mail seems to have been going missing from the mail room."

A low murmur ran around the room.

"Yes, indeed, you may look shocked," said Archangel Grace. "It's a worrying time for us all, and obviously someone must know what is going on. I just wanted to let you all know that I am taking it very seriously and intend to get to the bottom of it. If anyone knows anything, please come and talk to me about it."

And with that, she turned away, nodding over to the two angels with the harps, who started to play.

Ella was fizzing with excitement as the concerto came to an end and the assembly was over. She filed out with the others into the courtyard. The angels milled around, talking as they usually did. That day everyone was discussing the missing mail. Ella waited until everyone was there and then she pulled out her wand. Was this going to work? *Oh, please,* she prayed! She waved it three times, counting under her breath: "One . . . two . . . three!"

BOOM!

The glitter bomb exploded, sparkling letters forming in the air and multicolored glitter cascading down. . . . Only, it wasn't just the glitter that was flying through the air, but thick white marble dust. Ella let out a loud gasp as the glitter and dust cleared. The top half of the statue of Archangel Emmanuel had been blown to smithereens!

CHAPTER 7

Disaster!

THERE WAS A STUNNED SILENCE AS
the final sprinkles of glitter and marble
dust rained down. The words *Jappy Hirth Bessday* shone out in the air. Ella stood rooted to
the spot. She hadn't even gotten that right. . . .

"What the . . . ?" Archangel Grace ran forward, her bun bobbing on the back of her
head as she bent toward the wreckage. "A glitter bomb!" she cried. "And behind the statue
of Archangel Emmanuel. Who could have put

that there? What sort of angel would deliber-
ately try to destroy the ancient statue of our
most noble founder with a glitter bomb?"

Angel Gabriella joined her. "I'm sure there
must be a reasonable explanation for this."

"A reasonable explanation?" Archangel
Grace, who usually looked serene and calm,
was furious. "Enough is enough. First the
mail. Now this. Who is responsible for all

these things? Take responsibility right now!"

Ella wanted the ground to open and swallow her up. Everyone in the school was looking around. She wanted to speak up, but how could she? Her cheeks went bright red. She opened her mouth, but Poppy clapped a hand over it to silence her.

Ella gulped. If she admitted she was to blame, the others might get into trouble too. She knew they would try and take responsibility as well, even though it had been her idea to put the bomb by the statue—and add the extra powder. Oh, why hadn't she listened to them?

"Well, has no one got anything to say?" Archangel Grace demanded.

Ella felt herself hot and itchy under the collar. The other angels murmured around her.

"The angel responsible for this must come forward," insisted Archangel Grace. "If she doesn't, then the fireworks show tomorrow will be canceled!"

"Canceled?" all the angels gasped.

Archangel Grace nodded grimly. "And when the angel in question is found—and she *will* be found, have no doubt about it—I'll expel her from the school forever!"

A little gasp went around the crowd. Ella looked across at her friends in horror. Expelled!

"Now back to your dorms," snapped Archangel Grace. "I hope by lunchtime the culprit will have come forward and I shall be able to inform you that the show will take place as we had planned."

Ella hurried back to the dorm with the

others. Poppy and Tilly looked as shocked and pale as she did. Neither of them seemed to know what to say.

"Isn't it awful?" gasped Jess, as they shut the door behind them. "I can't believe someone set out to destroy the statue like that—I bet it is the same person who's been stealing the mail!"

"It's not!" blurted out Ella. "It was . . . it

was *me*! Well, the statue—I haven't been steal-ing the mail."

"You blew up the statue!" Jess gaped. "What?"

"I didn't mean to." Ella felt awful. "It was supposed to be a birthday surprise for you. The words were supposed to say *Happy Birthday, Jess.*"

Jess's mouth opened and closed.

"We were all involved," put in Poppy. "Tilly and I helped make the glitter bomb."

"But it was supposed to be a little bomb—just in here." Tilly gestured around the dorm. "What were you thinking, Ella?"

"I wanted to make it really special!" Ella said. "I wanted to let everyone know it was Jess's birthday and give her a real surprise. I must have put too much powder in."

"Way too much!" said Tilly.

"I'm sorry," said Ella, hot tears prickling her eyes. It had all gone so horribly wrong. "I'm just glad the message didn't work. If it had said *Happy Birthday, Jess,* as it was supposed to, then the Archangel would have guessed right away that it was us."

Jess went over and hugged her. "Oh, Ella." She shook her head. "It was a lovely thought. In fact"—she looked around at the others too—"it's the nicest thing that anyone has ever done for me. But now what are we going to do?"

"I'm going to have to go and admit it was me," said Ella. "I can't let everyone else get into trouble and have the show canceled."

"But you'll be expelled," protested Jess.

"I still have to go and confess," said Ella.

Tears fell down her cheeks. "Maybe I won't be expelled if I go and tell the truth."

"We'll come and take responsibility too," said Poppy.

Tilly nodded. "It is our fault as much as yours."

"No, it's not!" Ella shook her head. "You don't have to come."

"We do. We're all in this together. We're not going to let you take the blame," said Poppy, firmly. She hugged Ella and the other two joined in.

CRASH!

The door was shoved back with a mighty bang. The angels jumped as Primrose entered the room.

"Well, well, well," she sneered. "I suppose you thought no one would realize it was you, but I've guessed exactly what is going on. *Jappy Hirth Bessday*? It's Jess's birthday, isn't it? You told me in assembly," she told Ella. "I reckon you blew up the statue as a surprise. Well, I'm going to go and tell the Archangel right away."

"No, Primrose—no, you mustn't," Jess cried. "Please don't!"

But it was too late. Primrose was already off, flying down the hall.

"Come on!" gasped Jess. "We've got to stop her—before she gets to Archangel Grace!"

CHAPTER 8

An Unexpected Discovery

THE FOUR ANGELS CHARGED DOWN the hallway after Primrose, but she was so good at flying, she raced away from them.

"We've got to catch her!" gasped Poppy. "Ella, you're the fastest of us. You go on ahead!"

Ella beat her wings as fast as she could. She zoomed down the hallway and stairs, through the hall, and out into the courtyard. Primrose had just reached the Archangel and the teachers. "Archangel Grace! Archangel Grace! I know who did it!" Primrose cried in delight.

Archangel Grace and some of the other teachers were clustered around the ruined statue. They seemed to be peering inside. A bluebird was flying around their heads chirping loudly. They all turned.

Primrose's cheeks were flushed and her eyes triumphant. "I know who blew up the statue!" she exclaimed. "It was—"

"Me!" gasped Ella, screeching to a stop beside her.

Primrose looked crestfallen. "Ella wasn't going to admit it!" she told the teachers crossly. "She only came here just now because she knew I'd found out about her plan."

Archangel Grace handed something she was holding to Angel Seraphina. Her eyes were on Ella. "You destroyed the statue, Ella?" she said in astonishment.

Ella nodded. "I'm really, really sorry." The words tumbled out of her. "I didn't mean to blow up the statue. I promise I didn't! And I was coming to tell you, I really was. I didn't

want the fireworks show to be canceled and everyone to be punished because of me." Poppy, Tilly, and Jess landed beside her.

"Ella really was coming to take responsibility," Jess panted.

"I was going to confess too!" said Poppy.

"And me!" said Tilly. "Poppy and I helped Ella make the glitter bomb. It was a birthday surprise to cheer Jess up."

"I wanted it to rain glitter down on her and for everyone to know it was her birthday," said Ella.

"They should all be punished!" said Primrose, smugly.

"It was my idea to put it behind the statue," Ella said, shooting Primrose an angry look. "The others wanted to put it in the dorm. So punish me for destroying the statue, Archangel Grace. Please don't punish them."

"No, it's our fault too!" both Poppy and Tilly protested.

"Ella should be expelled!" Primrose said loudly.

Archangel Grace held up her hands. "Stop! All of you!"

The third graders all fell silent.

"So, let me get this straight," the head teacher said. "Ella, you and Poppy and Tilly made the glitter bomb but, Ella, you put it behind the statue?"

Ella nodded. "Because I wanted Jess's birthday surprise to be really big. You see, her birthday package hadn't arrived from her parents and . . . and . . ." She suddenly trailed off as she noticed that the teachers around the statue were all holding glittering packages and envelopes. "Packages . . ." she breathed. "There are lots of packages."

Her friends followed her gaze.

"Why have you got so many packages?" said Poppy.

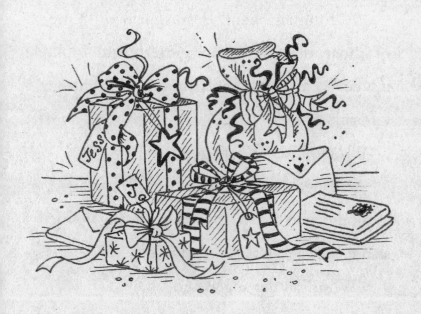

Jess gasped. "That one's from my mom and dad!" She pointed at a sparkly package in Angel Seraphina's hands. "I can see my mom's handwriting on the label."

Angel Seraphina read the label and smiled. "It is indeed for you, Jess—happy birthday." She handed the present to Jess, who promptly opened it.

"A fountain pen!" Jess squealed. "One of those that writes in glitter! And look, it's covered in stars and moons and glitter. Cherub-azing!"

Ella blinked. "What's going on?"

Archangel Grace smiled. "Well, Ella, it looks as though you did us a favor by blowing up the statue. We've found our mail thief."

"Who?" all the angels said.

"It was the bluebird," Archangel Grace replied.

"The bluebird!" Ella gasped.

"He must have been nesting inside the hollow statue," said Angel Gabriella, nodding. "Remember how I told you in class that bluebirds like nesting in strange places? Well, this bluebird had clearly decided to nest inside the statue—flying in through Archangel Emmanuel's mouth and nesting in the base."

The bluebird landed on her shoulder and chirped, his head tilted to one side.

"Bluebirds like sparkly things," remembered Ella. "You told us that too."

"Yes, and this one in particular seems to like them. We think he's simply been visiting the pigeonholes in the morning and picking up any packages or cards that caught his atten-tion. Naughty little creature!" Angel Gabriella shook her head.

The bluebird chirped at her boldly.

"So it wasn't an angel after all?" said Ella.

"No, thank goodness, and if you hadn't put your glitter bomb behind the statue, we might never have found out," said Archangel Grace. Her lips twitched into a smile. "Maybe we should be grateful to you, Ella Brown."

"Grateful!" spluttered Primrose. "Ella should be punished, Archangel. She's broken the statue—"

"Primrose, that's enough! The statue can be fixed with magic. Besides, aren't you forget-ting who the head teacher is here?" Archangel Grace said very sharply. Primrose subsided. "So,

Ella . . ." Archangel Grace turned to Ella again. "The question is, what should we do with you?"

Ella hung her head. What was her punishment going to be?

"What you did was clearly wrong, but it was obviously an accident," Archangel Grace said. "You were doing it for your friend, to cheer her up, and that shows real angel qualities. You have also demonstrated a real aptitude for glitter bomb making. Hmm . . ." She pressed her fingers together and regarded Ella. "Let me see. . . ."

"I really am very sorry," Ella said contritely. "I promise I'll never do it again."

Archangel Grace's eyes twinkled. "Then I think, my dear, we'll say no more about it."

"You mean I'm not going to be expelled?" Ella burst out in relief.

"No, no expulsions today," Archangel Grace said.

"I won't even take a halo stamp away, as you were trying to help a friend," Archangel Grace said, "but I will have to punish you. Weeding—the whole of the vegetable patch—and by bedtime this evening."

Ella nodded. She knew that it was more than fair.

"I'll help you," Tilly whispered, before turning to Archangel Grace. "So the fireworks show can definitely go ahead tomorrow?"

"It can indeed," said Archangel Grace. "In fact, maybe Ella would like to make another bomb, seeing as she is so good at it—only with Angel Gabriella's help this time. It can go off right at the end, as our final climax, after Primrose has performed. It seems a pity to waste such talent."

"But Archangel Grace, that's not fair! Ella really should lose a halo stamp as well for what she's done," cried Primrose.

Archangel Grace smiled and ruffled Primrose's hair. "Oh, Primrose, you heard what I said. Ella's going to weed the whole vegetable patch. That's quite enough. Besides, I think we've had enough excitement for one day." The head teacher paused. "Don't you?"

Ella looked up in the sky the next evening. Whizzes and bangs filled the air and flashes of light zoomed across the night. All of the third-grade angels were great in the show. As they whizzed back and forth with the lights there were *ooh*s and *aah*s from the crowd. The third graders' glitter bombs were mounted on trees for the finale and, with Angel Gabriella conducting, the third graders all waved their wands and counted to three. The bombs exploded, sending glitter and sparkles high into the sky. Ella flew to the side and waited to set off the massive glitter bomb she and Angel Gabriella had made that afternoon. It was going to be the very last thing in the show. First, Primrose had to appear in her starring role.

"I can't believe you're in the finale with me!" Primrose hissed by her side. "You should have been sent home. You should have been expelled . . ."

Ella just smiled to herself. She was so delighted by the show that even Primrose wasn't going to make her lose her temper that evening.

"You and your friends are never going to get enough halo stamps to even get sapphire halos, let alone make it to Guardian Angels. You—"

"Primrose...Primrose...Come on, or you'll miss your moment!" called Angel Celestine.

Ella giggled as Primrose rushed forward. She'd been so busy being horrible that she'd nearly missed her cue!

Primrose was clearly flustered and, as she flew through the sky, she got into a complete mess, missing the hoops of light that she was supposed to fly through.

There was a silence and then the crowd clapped half-heartedly but there was no rousing cheer. Primrose stormed off past Ella with a face like thunder.

"Oh dear, that wasn't a very impressive end to our show. I hope you can do better, Ella." Angel Celestine pushed Ella on. "Show everyone what the third-grade angels can do!"

Ella felt the butterflies in her stomach as she flitted forward with the glitter bomb in her arms, but once she was out there, she forgot everything and flew across the sky, making the perfect loop-the-loop.

"Hooray!" The cries echoed in her ears.

It was now or never. Ella threw the glitter ball up as high as she could. It soared into the air. Ella waved her wand three times and counted down. "One . . . two . . . three!" she shouted.

BANG!

The bomb exploded in the sky and the words formed in glittery pinks and purples.

There was a roar from the crowd. Ella smiled.

She paused for a moment to look down at all of the happy faces beneath her, before gently coming down to land beside her family and friends to the sound of rapturous

Guardian Angel Academy

applause. It was so good to see her parents again and she gave them a big hug. Poppy, Jess, and Tilly were doing the same to theirs. It was so lovely to see them all so happy, especially Tilly, who had been so homesick at the start of the term.

"Ella . . . Ella, that was fabulous." Her mother hugged her.

Her dad looked on proudly. "Who would have thought it?" he said. "My little Ella, the star of the show. My perfect angel."

Ella looked across at her friends. Tilly and Poppy raised their eyebrows and Jess chuckled. If only Ella's parents knew the truth! But they didn't say anything.

Ella left her parents for a moment to give her friends a big hug.

"We did it!" they cheered. "Hip, hip, hooray! We really did it. Now we get to go home for the the break too!"

"And then we'll be back at angel school for a lot more adventures—and to try and earn our sapphire halos," grinned Ella. "I can't wait!"

Read on for a sneak peek
at Ella's angel-tastic
adventures in:

MICHELLE MISRA

ANGEL
WINGS

Secrets and Sapphires

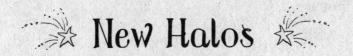

New Halos

"HAVE YOU HEARD THE NEWS?" WHISPERED Ella Brown in excitement, as she sat down next to her friend, Poppy, in morning assembly.

"What news?" Poppy demanded.

"It's angel-tastic! Someone in our grade has . . ."

"Sssh!" Tilly, one of their other friends, hushed them hastily. She nodded to the stage where Archangel Grace, the head of the Guardian Angel Academy, was waiting for silence.

Archangel Grace was a plump angel with wise eyes, enormous gossamer wings, and dark hair that was pulled back into a bun on the back of her head.

Ella fidgeted in frustration on the bench. She was longing to tell Poppy what she had just overheard on the way into the hall, but she didn't want to be lectured by Archangel Grace. She pushed her shoulder-length brown hair behind her ears and tried to concentrate.

"Good morning, angels," Archangel Grace said, smiling around at the school. "Now, before I make the morning announcements, I have some good news," she paused. "A third-grade angel has just completed her first halo card!"

"That's what I was going to tell you!" hissed

Ella, elbowing Poppy in the ribs, as excited gasps filled the air.

"Who is it?" whispered Poppy eagerly.

"I don't know!" Ella replied. All the angels at the academy had a halo card and were awarded halo stamps for good behavior. When an angel's halo card was completely filled in, the angel's halo would change color and her wings grow bigger. The white halos all the angels started with changed to sapphire, which changed to ruby and so on, all the way up until the final level was reached—the diamond level. Only the very best, most angelic angels ever got a diamond halo. Ella longed to have one.

She looked at the rest of the third graders, sitting on the bench. They all had white halos at the moment. Which of them had filled in

their card? She knew that it wasn't one of her best friends. Poppy, whose messy blonde curls were half hanging out of her ponytail and whose white dress was covered in splotches of ink, was lovely but she was very clumsy and scruffy—neither of which were perfect angel qualities. Tilly and Jess found it easier to get halo stamps—they were both quieter and more well-behaved—but Ella knew Jess needed another four halo stamps and Tilly another two. Ella touched her own halo card in her pocket and sighed. One thing was for sure—it definitely wasn't her. She still had ten halo stamps to get!

Halo stamps were awarded for being good and doing kind deeds and, although Ella liked to think she was kind, she definitely wasn't always good! She just couldn't help herself. She always tried her hardest, but somehow she couldn't stop herself from getting into trouble!

"Olivia Starfall, would you like to come up here?" Archangel Grace called over to where a sweet-looking angel with long dark hair and bright blue eyes was sitting, a little way down from Ella, her ankles crossed and her hands folded neatly in her lap.

Olivia! Of course! Ella wasn't surprised as Olivia stood up, blushing. Olivia was lovely— always happy to help out if you got stuck, but modest too. She could fly the most perfect loop-the-loop, her silver linings were careful and tidy, and her hair neatly combed. Ella smiled and applauded with the others when Olivia flew up to the stage, her tiny wings fluttering.

As she landed beside Archangel Grace, all of the angels cheered loudly. Well, nearly all of them—Ella caught sight of another angel at the far end of the third-grade bench who didn't look pleased at all. With her golden hair curled into ringlets, big blue eyes, and spotless uniform, you would have thought she was a perfect angel, if it wasn't for the scowl on her face. Primrose!

As Primrose leaned in to whisper to the red-haired angel beside her, she covered her mouth with her hand and her eyes narrowed spitefully. Ella sighed. She was sure that Primrose wasn't saying anything nice about Olivia. Ella turned back. Olivia was standing next to Archangel Grace now, her face pink with embarrassment. Archangel Grace raised her wand.

"Good shall be rewarded, virtue too, white halo change to shining blue...." She waved her wand in the air three times and a small cloud of

glittering silver angel dust cascaded down from it, landing on Olivia's halo. Instantly it turned to deep glowing sapphire and Olivia's white uniform became the pale blue of a spring sky.

A chorus of gasps and sighs filled the room.

"Wow, isn't that amazing!"

"She looks really beautiful!"

"Oh, I remember getting my sapphire halo when I was a third grader!"

Ella fluttered her own tiny little wings. She wanted to be up on that stage so badly. "I hope I get a sapphire halo soon," she breathed.

As Olivia flew back to her place, Archangel Grace called for silence again. "And now, on to another matter. A rather less happy one. As you all know, we make our very own angel dust here at the school. It comes from glitter flowers, which are very rare, and it has come to my attention that we're very low on stock. We've planted a new crop of flowers in the school greenhouse but it will take some time before they bloom. Isn't that right, Angel Celestine?" Archangel Grace turned to a pretty, dark-haired teacher who was seated with the other teachers at the back of the stage.

"It is indeed," said Angel Celestine, the gardening teacher. "The crop needs to flower before the glitter can be harvested, which can be tricky. Conditions need to be just right. Hopefully, we should be able to renew our supply of angel dust soon."

Archangel Grace nodded. "And in the meantime, the remaining angel dust must be used sparingly. As you all know, we were going to have the school Spring Picnic next weekend but I'm going to have to cancel it for the time being to save on magic."

"Oh no . . ." There were groans from around the room.

Ella had never actually been to the Spring Picnic but she'd heard all about it and had been looking forward to it too. Disappointment flooded through her.

Archangel Grace held up her hands again and silence fell. "I know that this will be a huge disappointment to you and I'm really sorry for that, but I am sure you can all understand that we must be sensible. If we run out of angel dust, we won't be able to do any angel magic and that would be a catastrophe."

The angels in the room nodded understandingly.

"We shall have the picnic when the flowers can be harvested," said Archangel Grace. "In the meantime if anyone would like to help out in the greenhouses, looking after the plants, then I am sure Angel Celestine would be very grateful. Now, let us all stand and sing Glad Tidings and Silver Linings."

When assembly was over, Ella filed out of the hall with the other angels. As soon as they were away from the teachers' watchful eyes, she crowded around with her friends.

"Isn't it amazing about Olivia?" burst out Tilly.

"Just glittersome!" said Poppy.

"It'll be us next," joined in Jess, flicking her long dark ponytail over her shoulder.

"Well, maybe you and Tilly," sighed Ella. "But Poppy and I have quite a few more halo stamps to get, don't we, Poppy?"

But Poppy wasn't listening. She was looking at the other side of the room where Primrose was now standing with her arm linked through Olivia's. "Primrose is unbelievable," she said, shaking her head. "Yesterday, she made a fuss because she didn't want to sit with Olivia in forgetting spell class because she said Olivia was boring. Now, she's acting like they're best friends!"

Primrose fawned as people came up to congratulate the other girl. "Oh, I always knew darling Livvy would be the first to get her sapphire halo," she said loudly. "She's wonderful, isn't she?"

Olivia gave Primrose a very surprised look.

Ella snorted. "If getting a sapphire halo means having Primrose hanging around, then maybe I don't want to fill my halo card after all."

"Ssh! They're coming over!" hissed Jess.

Olivia headed in their direction, with Primrose holding tightly to her arm.

"Congratulations, Olivia," Ella smiled.

"Thanks, Ella," said Olivia shyly. "I can't believe I was the first to get my sapphire halo. It was a real fluke."

"I was just saying how amazing Olivia's sapphire dress and halo look on her, don't you agree?" Primrose gushed. "It's cherub-azing!"

"Er, thank you," said Olivia, clearly flustered by Primrose's attention. "Well, I've got to get something from my dorm. I'll . . . um, see you later." She managed to extract herself from Primrose's grasp and hurried away.

"Don't be long! I'll save you a seat in class!" Primrose called sweetly after her.

"What's going on, Primrose?" Ella demanded. "Since when have you saved Olivia a seat in class?"

Primrose gave her a wide-eyed look. "I'm just being thoughtful."

"Thoughtful!" spluttered Ella. "You've never said two words to Olivia before but suddenly she gets a sapphire halo and you're her new best friend. I bet you just want to hang around with her now because everyone's giving her loads of attention."

"What a mean thing to say!" Primrose looked shocked. "And when I was only trying to do a kind deed. You know the School Handbook says perfect angels are always kind." She gave Ella a snooty look. "Though why I should expect you to know anything about being the perfect angel, I don't know.

How many halo stamps do you still have to get before your card is full, Ella? Is it five? Six? Oh, sorry, I think it's ten, isn't it? Ten!" She rolled her eyes. "And I need ... hmm, just four. Well, never mind. I'm sure you'll complete your first halo card one day—even if the rest of us have our diamond halos by then! Now, please excuse me or I will be late for class."

Putting her nose in the air, she flew away.

Ella let out a frustrated exclamation. "Halos and wings! Primrose is so annoying!"

"Calm down," said Tilly, putting a hand soothingly on Ella's arm. "She's not worth getting upset over."

"Definitely not," declared Poppy. "You'll fill your halo card up quickly. We all will. Who cares who gets there first?"

"Soon we'll all have sapphire halos like Olivia," said Jess happily. "But Primrose was right about one thing—we'd better not be late for Angel Gabriella or we'll lose some of the halo stamps we've already got!"

"Come on!" she cried, whizzing into the air. "Let's go!"